I Am The Streets

Book One

T.L. Joy

www.mahoganypublications.com

Table of Contents

Prologue

They say you have to crawl before you walk, but sometimes you get too tired of crawling. I had to make a way out of no way, but the fast life wasn't for me. I was too pretty to be a stripper, and too smart to be a prostitute. So what else could I do? I didn't live in a town where I could access celebrities and be a groupie hoe. Instead, I lived in a city where men ruled the strip clubs and used them as a back-door prostitution ring. Girls as young as 14 were strippers turned into prostitutes. There had to be changes in the city. Someone had to do it, but everyone was scared to step out and change it.... So shit, I chucked up my fear and decided that I had to change the game. What is my name? I don't have one of those anymore. I lost my identity in the streets.... Just call me Lady Hustla'.

Prologue

Chapter One

"Why be a model when I can be the owner of the agency?" was what I said when niggas used to ask me if I wanted to be, or was, a model. I was 24 years old, Spelman University alumna, and was as conceited and arrogant as I wanted to be. Compared to all the girls back in my hometown, I did the damn thing! Graduated from high school, landed scholarships, and dipped off to college. I did it all by myself and didn't have to strip or suck a dick to help me. I left and never looked back. I went from the hood to high class, rocking my pearls, diamonds, and Christian Louboutins, and dating only the cream of the crop. Employed as a paralegal by the top law firm in Atlanta, I made enough money to own my own condo and drive my little BMW. Yeah, a girl was living large at a young age... but all that changed when shit hit the fan.

"Good morning, Mr. Spencer," I greeted as I walked into the Spencer & Barring law firm on a Monday morning. "Good morning, gorgeous." He smiled. For a 58 year old, Mr. Spencer looked damn good. Women loved him due to his identical appearance to the charming Denzel Washington. Employees here would die to sleep with him; half of them probably did, but not me. I'm a firm believer in hard work, and I would never suck a dick to make my way to the top. There are other ways around it, called using your sex appeal, wheeling them in and then smacking 'em with the brains.

"I have to go to a meeting in Toronto in two hours, so it will be an easy day at the office. You won't have me working you like a dog." He winked. I wanted to throw up at his sexual advances; instead, I just smiled and nodded. "That is fine with me, sir," I replied.

"Ok, well let me get the move on.... See you later Kristen," he ended as he walked away. Kristen was my new name, to help portray the new me. I came from Na'Tiva from the hood of Akron to Kristen in the moving city of Atlanta.

As I sat at my cherry-wood desk, I admired myself in my personal mirror. Smooth golden brown skin, hazel eyes, and natural bra-strap length hair that was dyed jet black and styled in feather curls. With the looks, and a curvaceous body to die for, I looked like the black Marilyn Monroe! I played her role well, embracing the dainty and feminine ways to make men feel manly and get whatever I wanted, without using sex... just using sex appeal. The loud ring of the phone blared, interrupting my "me" time.

"Spencer and Barring office," I answered. "Hello, Miss Na'Tiva." The voice of my mother traveled through my phone. "Mom! What are you doing calling my work phone? Didn't I tell you about that?" I interrogated.

"Oh, chile, be quiet! This is ya' mama callin' you, not some fluezy off the street," she snapped.

"What do you want?" I sighed.

"Well other than calling to hear my baby's voice over the phone, I called to tell you that you need to come home," she said as her tone became serious.

"Umm... that option is slim to none, next!" I scoffed.

"I'm serious, 'Tiva," she said, calling me by my hood nickname.

"Your little sister got caught up in some mess and I'm worried about her." She stressed her concern as I rolled my eyes in disgust.

"Momma, my sister is a dick suckin', trick lovin' stripper, getting caught up in some mess comes with the territory," I spat.

"Some people aren't as blessed as you are, 'Tiva. It's not nice to judge others because of their hustle," she said calmly. "But I guess since you're Kristen... you wouldn't understand it since you got that stick up your ass now," she jabbed.

"I'm not about to sit here and go back and forth with you, Momma. I love you, but I'm never going back to Akron. I left that shithole of a city and I'm never coming back," I said sternly.

"Ok, little miss priss, if that's how you feel, then fine! I will handle it myself, and if something happens to her, then it's on you," she replied angrily.

"Whatever, good-bye," I retorted as I hung up the phone. I swear that woman can pinch a nerve.

As quickly as I encountered that phone call was as quickly as I erased it from my mind. Over time I learned how to gain amnesia quick when it came to anything pertaining to my past in Akron. I went through hell living there and I don't want to go through it anymore. I quickly snapped back to my new reality and went on about my business.

As my shift was ending, I became excited about my dinner with my sexy boyfriend Damien. He was finally in town this week, and any time I could get with him was greatly cherished since he was the star of his NFL team, and the time we got to spend together was limited.

While I took a quick break, I decided to give Damien a call.

"Hello." His deep voice filled my ears.

"Hey baby. Just calling to see how everything's going," I said sweetly.

"It's not going good. I'm going to have to cancel our plans for dinner." He sighed.

"Are you serious?" I snapped.

"I'm sorry babe, but Coach wants us to do some extra training tonight and the rest of the week is booked. How about Friday. I promise I won't bail on you then," he said, causing me to roll my eyes in annoyance.

"Fine. Friday it is." I sighed.

"Good. I'll see you then. Love you baby." I could hear the smile in his voice.

"Love you too," I replied before we hung up. It seemed as if every time he was in town he would always blow me off and give me at most two days of his time. Even though I loved this man and the things he did for me, I got tired of being brushed off whenever we made plans.

I took a deep breath as I sat back in my leather office chair. Even though most of my life was what one would deem "perfect," my love life and my relationship was far from perfect.

The rest of the week continued on, consisting of work, graduate school, and nights out into the Atlanta social scene. It was finally Friday, and after a long day of graduate classes and work, I walked into my condo ready to unwind. Slipping into my sexy red teddy and some fire-red pumps, I poured two glasses of chardonnay, anticipating Damien's arrival.

Trey Songz played in the background, getting me in the mood for what was about to come. I had it all planned out until my phone rang. Looking down at the caller ID, I sighed in annoyance. Why the hell was my little sister Na'Tya calling me, don't she have a pole to strip on?

"What do you want?" I said displeasingly.

"I—I—I—I," she stammered in between cries.

"What?" I spat.

"Momma got shot!" she said, piercing into my heart. It felt as though everything went into slow motion. I couldn't even mutter a word. "She's dead.... she's dead... mama's dead, 'Tiva.... Someone shot her to death." Na'Tya cried through the phone.

I couldn't believe it. The woman who gave me life, the woman who took care of everyone in the community, who was well loved, was dead? I just talked to her on Monday, how could she have possibly died four days later? Tears rolled down my face uncontrollably. I guess I'll finally do what she wanted me to do. "I'm comin' to Akron! I'll call you when I get there," I finally said before hanging up the phone and packing up my shit.

Chapter Two

"Well look at little miss priss! Here she go walking in here like she is the head bitch in charge!" my sister yelled outlandishly in the airport. I winced at the site of her long, two-toned blond and red weave against her caramel skin. Her eyebrow and Marilyn Monroe piercing caused her to look different compared to the sweet little sister that I used to know. Na'Tya was known as "Diamond Dior" on the streets, and she was like a celebrity, bigger than rapper Nicki Minaj, in the city of Akron. With the money she gained from stripping, Na'Tya bought 36 double D cups and a ridiculous Brazilian ass to match. Not only was she stripping, but she made a brand for herself by modeling, posing for wanna-be hood rappers' album covers and party flyers, and making her own porno flicks. I had to give her some props for hustling, doing more than just stripping. But it was a sad sight to see my beautiful sister turn into a ghetto-fabulous street celebrity.

"Ugh, do you really have to be outlandish in a public place?" I rolled my eyes as she embraced me in a hug. "Girl, you know I missed you. It's been years since I last seen you." Na'Tya smiled as she stood back and took a good look at me. "Ooo and you got thick too! Who's been spreadin' them hips?" She laughed.

"I don't think that is appropriate considering the circumstances of why I'm here," I declined as I grabbed my suitcases.

"I guess you want to be all uptight huh?" she replied, sensing my disposition.

"No one is uptight, 'Tya. I'm just tired, irritated, and ready to get some rest! Mom is dead and we have a lot of shit to do for the funeral, so can we save all the reunited talk for later and just focus on the important shit?" I snapped.

"Whateva', if that's what you want then that's how it will be." Na'Tya rolled her eyes and contained her temper before we headed toward the parking lot.

Silence filled the car as we drove through the city. It had been years since I'd been back here, and I certainly dreaded the return. Yet I couldn't lie, I did have some good times in Akron. School dances, many crushes on boys who were two grades higher than me, girl talk over the telephone, summer flings, and my first love. Those were the things I cherished in my life; those were the things I would always hold on to when I thought of Akron.

"We're here," Na'Tya announced with attitude. "Since you don't want to talk about small remedial things, I guess I won't tell yo' ass about B-Moore wanting to see you while you are down here," she continued before she hopped out the car.

"B-Moore..." I repeated. I hadn't heard that name since I was seventeen years old. "What do you mean B-Moore wants to see me? You know I don't want people knowing I'm down here, 'Tya," I lectured as I followed her into her condo.

"Too bad!" she exclaimed as she threw off her heels and plopped onto her black loveseat.

"I swear you are nothing but a pain in my ass," I fumed.

"I'll be that, but it ain't my fault that your ex-boo is out here looking and asking about you. You're the one who left him high 'n' dry so you could go and be all bougie and act like an uppity college bitch," she spat, hitting me with a low blow. "As fine as he is, I would never leave his sexy—" she started, but I quickly cut her off.

"There is nothing wrong with a woman who wants to better her life. You act like it's wrong of me to want nothing but the best for myself. That's what's wrong with you and these ghetto-ass girls out here, you got your priorities all fucked up! Chasing after loser-ass hood niggas and only wanting fast cash while you steady live off the government. Well newsflash! That is not the way the world works. You will get nowhere in life chasing niggas and fast money. Sure you can travel, and maybe move out the hood, but intellectuals and successful hard workers like my colleagues and myself will only laugh and mock at dumb fucks like you. You are nothing but a joke to us. Ignorant-ass people with fucked up priorities, living ghetto-fabulous lives. You're like the scum on the bottom on my Giuseppes," I scoffed.

"So go ahead, Diamond Dior! Keep stripping, making porno flicks, and thinking you are hot shit, 'cause at the end of the day, no real successful, intellectually challenged man will want you as a wife; instead you will be just another stripper hoe that he fucks and throws away," I jabbed as I folded my arms and smirked at her.

"You think you know everything 'Tiva, but in reality, you don't know jack shit about the streets!" she said as she got in my face. "Your ass wouldn't last two minutes out here with your fuckin' judgmental, uppity ass. Thinkin' you're better then all of us... but in reality you are no different from all the rest of us females out here. You done sucked 'n' fucked hood niggas. Hell you even got pregnant, did you not?" Na'Tya finished, hitting me with another low blow from my past.

"How dare you bring that up!" I said, getting steaming mad.

"Mmmhmm, yo' ass went right to the clinic like the rest of us did. So as far as I'm concerned, you are no different from any other hood chick out here." She smirked.

Angry at the blast from my past, I walked away from her before I would do something crazy... like murder her bitch ass! "Fuck you 'Tya!" I shouted as I began to grab my bags.

She laughed in response. "Yeah, don't sit here and act all sweet 'n' innocent, hoe! I know you. I been with you our whole lives, and I seen the shit you did. You were far from a fucking angel back when you lived in Akron, so you can stop with that bullshit act you are trying to pull," she ranted. As she continued to go on and on, I tuned her out and made my way up the stairs to the guest room. This was going to be a long week staying with this bitch!

Chapter Three

"I'm sorry to have to meet you under these circumstances, Ms. Davis. Your mother was such a big influence in this community with her youth support services," Detective Willis began as we walked into his office. I had just viewed my mother's grotesque body at the morgue, and I wanted answers. I wanted justice! I know that we didn't have the best relationship, but they didn't have to do her like that. Almost twenty rounds in her body, for what?

"I want to know what happened and who did this to her," I commanded.

A brooding expression covered his brown face as he took off his thick glasses and let out a deep sigh.

"It appeared to be a breaking and entering since her TV was missing and her was jewelry stolen. We believe Mrs. Davis put up a fight due to the bruising of her knuckles, but the altercation was put to an end when the suspect shot her to death. That's what turned the breaking and entering into a homicide. Unfortunately, we didn't find any evidence leading us to a prime suspect. There were no witnesses that may have seen someone in the apartment building that looked suspicious. But you know they have a code of no snitching, which is prevalent in Akron," he explained.

I rolled my eyes in disgust. *Fuck their code!* I wanted to scream out. Yet instead, I held back my tears of anger as I sat back and let Detective Willis provide more information about my mother's murder.

The pang of guilt hit me like a ton of bricks as I left the office. If only I had listened to her when we were on the phone, if only I had just came home sooner, she would still be alive! Tears streamed down my face as I sped down the highway toward 'Tya's house. My mother didn't deserve to die like that. Shit, she didn't even deserve to die at all. She was only 56 and perfectly healthy! She was taken way too soon all because some hood niggas wanted a little money, a funky old-ass TV, and some jewelry?

This was exactly why I left this fucking city. After my best friend Shanae got raped and murdered in an abandoned building during my senior year of highschool, I knew it was time to go. First my friend, now my mother? This was all too much!

Once I pulled up into 'Tya's driveway, I made a promise to myself that I would hold it together for the sake of my mother. I want to give her the proper funeral she deserved, and the least I could do was be cordial with my sister. Even if she has her moments, I don't need to snap back at her. Momma would have wanted this.... This was exactly the thing she'd been asking me to do: spend time with my sister and make amends. That's the least I can do.

I took a deep sigh as I sucked up my tears. It was finally time that I put myself to the side, just for the sake of my late mother. I grabbed my belongings and made my way into Na'Tya's house.

"Where the fuck you been?" 'Tya asked as she sat in her dining room, rolling up a blunt with three other niggas that I never seen before. It took all I had to stop myself right before I said something smart to her.

"I went to check up on Momma's case. I talked to Detective Davis at his office," I explained.

"Oh." Her face changed to a sullen expression. "How'd that go?" she asked.

"Not good." I sighed. "I don't want to interrupt you and your company, so I'mma go upstairs and take it easy. We can talk later," I continued as I glanced at her three friends.

"You sure you don't want to take a hit, 'Tiva? I know you used to be the cheefin' queen back in the day." 'Tya smiled with the finished blunt in her hand.

I smiled back. "Naw, I'm good 'Tya."

"Ok, girl. I'll come holla at you lata' then," she replied.

I nodded my head in response and made my way upstairs. *At least that was a good start. I think I can survive being cordial with my sister after all*, I thought to myself as I plopped on the bed to get ready to take a long-needed nap.

~~~

Despite our many issues, Na'Tya and I worked together to plan our mother's funeral. My bloodshot eyes were hidden behind my black tinted Celine sunglasses as we walked into the large Cathedral church. Everyone in the room was dressed in all white, my mother's favorite color. Red roses surrounded my mother's closed casket, as the choir sung their hearts out. My body trembled as I got closer to her casket. I couldn't even see her face one last time! 'Tya gripped my hand harder as we got ready to sit in the front pew, not even four feet away from our mother's body. Everything just seemed too surreal. I never thought I would see this day coming.

Everyone from our family and the majority of the community filled the church. They lined up to walk up to the casket and pay their respects. I tried to stay strong as each and every one gave 'Tya and I
~~~

hugs, but as I stood there in the familiar embrace of the man that I had once loved, the man who comforted me in my most trying times... I lost all control.

“Whyyyyyy?” I wailed out in deep pain.

“Why you, Momma? Why you?” I said in between sobs. I always said that I would never cry in front of people. But you would be surprised what you would do if you were in that situation. No one can predict that. No one knew the pain and guilt I felt over my mother’s death.

“It’s ok,” Brandon, aka B-Moore, whispered in my ear as he held me tightly and rubbed my back. His voice was soothing to my soul. The one person who understood me. The one person who actually knew how I feel since his mother died many years ago.

I couldn't even see his face. Just hear his voice and feel his touch, which was somewhat comforting for me. Soon, many people rushed up to me to hug and comfort me.

I took a deep sigh and moved back. This wasn't about me. Today was our mother's day, a day to celebrate her life. "I'm ok now... let's just get started," I managed to say out loud.

Just as I suggested, everyone went to their seats and the funeral began. I sat in my seat and quietly rocked my body side to side to help calm me down, whereas 'Tya was a hot mess! Worse than me!

"Momma! No, Momma, no!" she yelled as she hopped out her seat and ran to our mother's casket.

"Take me with you! I don't know how I'mma live without you, Momma." She broke down on the floor and began crying and shaking uncontrollably.

"I don't know if I can do this anymore," she stuttered.

Our cousin Big Jeff rushed to her side and helped pick her up. She wailed deeply on his shoulder as he picked her up and took her out to the back of the church. I never seen 'Tya like this, even when daddy died. As the pastor resumed his speech, I made my way to the back of the church building to comfort my sister. I hugged her until she calmed down, and we went back to the temple together.

After the burial of our mother's casket, we went back to the church dining hall to have dinner. I sat at the table in silence until I felt a hand on my shoulder.

"I'm sorry for your loss." The deep and soothing voice filled my ears. I turned around only to see Brandon standing there. His 6'3" frame towered over me as his intense, light brown eyes pierced my soul. I couldn't help but be taken aback by his physical appeal. His smooth caramel skin and jet-black waves gleamed under the light, and his facial hair was trimmed to perfection. I hadn't seen this man in over four years, but every feeling that I had for him rushed back in that instant.

"Tha-thank you Brandon," I replied. He sat down in the chair next to me and grabbed my hand.

"I know that you breaking down in the church was unlike you. You probably were surprised yourself," he said.

"I was!" I lightly chuckled.

"Yeah... but it is expected, La'tiva. I was a wreck when my mother died... you remember," Brandon reminded me.

"I know." I looked away for a moment, holding back a tear. "I remember."

"You can't always be strong, 'Tiva. I know it's hard for you to even have a moment like that and break down, but we all go through it. It's ok, it's good to let it out..." Brandon stopped and stared at me. Our eyes met and I nodded my head in agreement.

"You're right," was all I could say.

"If you need anything, need any support. or just want to talk... call me. I'm here for you 'Tiva," Brandon explained as he handed me a business card with his name and number on it.

"Thanks, Brandon," I said as I took his card and put it in my clutch.

"All right, I got to get back to work, but I had to stop by and show my respect. Call me, ok?" he asked as he got up from his seat.

"Ok." I smiled.

"Now that's what I like to see: a smile on your face! Mission complete," he joked, causing us to both laugh. "I hope to hear from you soon," he continued. I nodded my head in response as he gripped my shoulder and walked away.

I couldn't help but smile. He was the only man to have that effect on me, to make me feel at ease in the worst situations. That was one of the reasons why I fell in love with him. Snapping myself out of my little trance, I got up and began to make my way around the room and properly greet and comfort my family.

~~~
~~~

"Aww! I seen you over there with B-Moore!" 'Tya exclaimed as we drove home hours later. We spent most of the time talking to family members and friends of the family that we hadn't had time to even chat with each other.

"Look at that smile on yo' face. Reunited and it feels so good, huh?" she joked.

"You're so silly, 'Tya." I shrugged off.

"Girl, please! You can't even deny it. We may not have been around each other in a while, but I know my sister! I know when B-Moore done made you feel good and at ease. When are you going to see him again?"

"I don't know," I replied, puzzled.

I was having an inner conflict with myself. I didn't want to go back to my past. Brandon was a part of my past living here in Akron, and I for damn sure did not want to rekindle an old flame and have a reason to be attached and want to stay here. Then again, I knew he would be a good friend and support system during this rough time. My boyfriend is busy training for the championship game, and I didn't want to wear his ears out about my problems.... He wouldn't understand anyway.

"'Tiva, you better call that man! I mean shit, you ain't about to be out here for that long anyway. Who knows when your ass is even coming back. So shit, the least you could do is talk to him and give him some damn closure since you left his ass high 'n' dry before you went to college," 'Tya explained, snapping me out of my thoughts.

"You got a point..."

"I know I do!" she snapped.

"Whatever, 'Tya." I laughed. "Worrying about me and mine. What about your love life, huh?" I said, reversing the attention on her.

"Fuck all that! I'm about this money, baby!" Tya declared as she zoomed down the highway. "Love don't pay no bills around here. If a nigga want to make me his wifey, he gotta' come correct and amaze the hell out of me," she continued.

"So I guess yo' ass is celibate with cobwebs on the cooch, huh? I would've never guessed it, 'Tya." I laughed, causing her to look at me with the side eye.

"Bitch, what? I still get the dick every now and then! I just don't have time to deal with a nigga every day. Like I said, love don't pay no bills, and good dick is a dime a dozen. I won't let dick turn me into a kept bitch!" she continued.

"Well excuse the hell out of me!" I exclaimed. "I learn something new every day," I joked.

"Whatever, sis!" She laughed. "Let's just get home and have some drinks. Especially after a day like today," she suggested.

"I'm down for that, cause we definitely need a drink." I smiled.

"Hell yeah!" she exclaimed before she started dancing to the music on the radio, making me laugh.

It was good to finally be back on good terms with my sister, to talk to her and laugh with her like the old days. I knew my mother was smiling down from heaven at us. She finally got what she wanted.

Chapter Four

"I know that you may already know the terms of this life insurance policy, but I wanted to have you here today so we can go over this and your mother's will," said the pale-faced man dressed in a black suit across from 'Tya and me. It had only been a couple of days after our mother's funeral, but there were still some important things that had to be handled.

"According to your mother's life insurance policy, she listed both of you as her beneficiaries, so you will both get an equal split of the one million dollar payout. As far as the terms of Mrs. Davis's will, she designated that $150,000 from her savings will go to La'Tiva to help cover her student loans," Mr. Corgan explained, leaving me in shock.

Although 'Tya and I fronted the money for our mother's funeral, I had no idea that our mother had a life insurance policy, let alone a will. Then again, I hadn't talked to her in years, which is more of the reason why I'm shocked that she included me in her will.

"Were there any other designations that she included for me?" 'Tya asked with pleading eyes.

"Umm..." Mr. Corgan said as he scanned the document in his hand. "The only designation that she has listed for you in her will is to own her Kia Sorento," he continued.

"A Kia Sorento? What the fuck am I going to do with that?" 'Tya snapped. "And there was nothing else?" she asked as she sat on the edge of her seat.

"I'm sorry, Ms. Davis"—he looked up at her—"but there is nothing else designated for you in her will."

"What the fuck!" She stood up full of anger. "I can't believe this bullshit! I've been there for her, even when there was no one else by her side, and this is how she does me? She gives the majority of her damn money to the daughter who damn near disowned her, and all she can give me is a funky-ass Kia Sorento? I got my own Lexus SUV and a Benz, what the fuck am I going to do with her shit?" she continued as she grabbed her belongings.

"I don't want to hear anything else. I'm done with this shit! Meet me out at the car when you done with bullshit, 'Tiva," my sister yelled as she trailed out of the office, leaving me speechless at her reaction.

I understood that she was upset about how the money got divided, but she is still walking out with $500,000. It ain't about the money, cause at the end of the day, our mother was six feet under, and I would rather have her alive and well over money any day. Yet, 'Tya may see things differently since she feels like there is favoritism coming into play.

"I'm so sorry about my sister's outburst, Mr. Corgan," I apologized.

"No problem. I'm used to dealing with all kinds of emotions when I explain terms to families. I even had a man punch me one time," he shared.

"Oh wow! That extreme?" I asked.

"Yes. You'd be surprised." He chuckled. "Things like this are very touchy."

"I understand that." I sighed. "Was there anything else listed in her will?" I continued.

"Ah, yes," he said as he looked over the paper. "She did have some stocks and bonds that she would like to have transferred to you as well," Mr. Corgan concluded.

"Ok." I nodded. I never even knew that she invested in stocks and bonds. I guess she was smarter than I thought.

"Any questions or concerns, Ms. Davis?" he asked, breaking my thoughts.

"Uh, no. Not at this time," I answered as I grabbed my purse.

"Great! The payout will disperse by the end of this week," he explained as we both stood up.

"Ok. Well thank you for everything," I said while shaking his hand.

"No problem, ma'am. If you need anything else, just call me."

"Ok," I concluded before walking out of his office. Since 'Tya was so heated from the discussion,

I decided to leave out the fact that Mama left me her stocks and bonds.

"So what the fuck he say?" she asked as I stepped into her car.

"He just said that the payout will come by the end of this week," I replied.

"Oh, ok..." was all 'Tya could say as she threw her black and mild out the window and started up the car. I knew that the best thing to do was keep my mouth shut while she was this upset. Nothing I could say would make the situation better. So we drove in silence the whole ride home.

~~~

As soon I plopped onto my bed, 'Tya made no hesitation to call up some of her people to come over and spark a blunt with her. That seemed to be
~~~

her royal tradition at the end of a long day. Yet, I didn't feel like being bothered by random niggas and sketchy females, so I grabbed my phone and dialed his number.

"Hello." Brandon's deep voice filled my ears.

"Hey.... It's 'Tiva," I said softly.

"Oh hey, 'Tiva. I'm surprised you called."

"Why are you surprised? You're the one who suggested me to call you."

"Don't mean you'll actually do it." He chuckled.

"Well I did.... So what are you doing tonight? Did you have plans?" I asked.

"Actually, I don't have any plans for tonight, but you can become a part of my plans," he said, causing a smile to creep over my face.

"I would like that."

"Dinner tonight at eight?" he suggested.

"Yes. Where at?" I asked.

"How about I surprise you. Just be ready when I come pick you up. You're staying over at 'Tya's place, right?"

"Yeah. You know the address?"

"I definitely know the address. She used to date my boy Cj a while ago, and I had to come over there and pick his drunk ass up after their arguments," he explained.

"Why am I not surprised by that." I laughed. "But I'll be ready by eight."

"Good. I'll see you then."

"See you then," I replied before hanging up the phone. A smile stayed plastered on my face as I took a shower and got ready for the night. I don't know why he had that effect on me after so many years, but he did.

I slipped into my sexy red Hermès dress with my matching red spiked Christian Louboutin heels. I stood in the mirror and admired myself as I applied my makeup and curled my hair to perfection. If looks could kill tonight, I would cause a massacre based on how good I was looking!

"'Tiva! Someone is here for you," my sister yelled out from downstairs. I quickly grabbed my spiked leather clutch and made my way downstairs only to see Brandon standing there looking sexy as ever. Dressed in a black button-up, black slacks and shoes, and a red tie, this man was nothing short of amazing. He came a long way from baggy jeans, the latest Jordans, and jerseys. He was now rockin' diamond studded Rolex and cufflinks. Looking sexy and professional.

"Well damn. You're beautiful as ever," he said as he embraced me in a hug.

"Thank you." I smiled. "And aren't you looking handsome."

"Well I try, I try." He smiled.

"Will ya'll get the fuck outta my house with that corny shit," 'Tya yelled out from the kitchen table.

"Ugh! Whatever, 'Tya. I'll see you when I get back," I said as we headed toward the front door.

"Shit, if you come back. Go head girl! I'll see you later," she joked, causing me to shake my head.

"Let's just go," I said to Brandon before walking outside.

As soon as I laid eyes on his all-white 2015 Bentley Continental GT V8S, I was in awe.

"Wow, you have changed up on me." I smiled as I walked over to his car.

"Life has been treating me good." He chuckled as he opened the car door for me.

"I see that." I laughed as I slid into his car and sunk down on his black and white leather interior. I've dated many wealthy men, but seeing Brandon, my ex from Akron, owning this car had me flabbergasted. *What the fuck has he been doing to get this car?* was all I could think as we drove to our destination. Even with our small talk on the way, I still wondered what his occupation was.

Once we arrived at *Dante Boccuzzi,* an upscale restaurant in Akron, I couldn't help but laugh.

"Nice choice," I said to Brandon as we followed the waiter to our table.

"Only for you," he said, flashing me his Colgate smile.

After we got to our table, I shared with him about my life as a student and paralegal in Atlanta. Once I was done, I couldn't help but ask... "So what do you do now? I remember that you use to have so many lofty dreams and aspirations back in high school, so where did your journey to success end up?"

He took a sip of his wine before speaking. "You were right. I did have so many dreams and aspirations back then, but I tried to do it all until one finally stuck. I own a large chain of C&B auto and tow shops across the state of Ohio. I took over pop's old auto shop after he passed and decided to think bigger. So, I made it happen and we are raking in all the profits," he explained, leaving me purely impressed.

"I love it!" I gleamed. "I love how much you've progressed since then."

"Yes. We came a long way from being just two teenagers out here trying to make a name for ourselves in Akron," he replied.

"That is true." I smirked.

"So let's make a toast..." Brandon purposed before holding up his glass. "To love, to success, and to our future endeavors."

"Cheers," I said before clinking our glasses together. Our eyes locked as we sipped on our drinks, and at that moment, I knew that I wanted him.

As we sat and ate our meals, we reminisced on old times of us being together.

"You know yo' ass was bad! Sneaking out late at night to meet me and get it in at the park." He smiled, causing me to laugh.

"Don't try to play me like that, B-Moore!" I said, calling him by his old nickname. "You know I was sweet and innocent."

"Hell naw! Yo' ass was nowhere near innocent!" he exaggerated.

"Whatever!"

"But foreal. We did have some good times. High school life with the only girl I loved. Can't get no better than that," he said, calming down. "A nigga was hurt when you left," he continued.

"I didn't want to leave." I sighed.

"I know." He nodded as his eyes left mine.

The pang of guilt hit me like a ton of bricks. At one time in my life this was the man I loved, the man that I would do anything for. Now, here we were sitting before each other after many years later, and all I could think about was how I wanted to lay in his arms again. To feel that feeling of being safe and loved again, instead of being just someone's temporary lover whenever he was in town... like Damien.

"But we are here now, grown and sexy." He paused as his light brown eyes grazed my body. "So let's have a clean slate and make the most of it while we are here." He smiled.

"Yes." I let out a sigh of relief. "Let's make the most of it," I continued, hoping that we could possibly rekindle our old flame.

Chapter Five

Introducing Na'Tya

While everyone was up in my house laughing and talking, I sat in my chair and thought about how fucked up my day has been. After all I've done for me and my momma while 'Tiva was out there living the life of a prissy college bitch, all I got was a small amount of money and a fucking Kia Sorento? I knew Mama always had favoritism for Na'Tiva, but she took that shit too far! My blood began to boil as I thought about how I got up in this fucked up situation.

Flashback:

Once my sister left to go start her life down in Atlanta, she left me and Mama out here to fend for ourselves. I was only seventeen years old, barely able to graduate since my grades were fucked up due to stress of my mama losing her job, and my sister leaving me here to be the only one bringing in money for the household. No matter what it was, I was willing to do any and everything I had to do to get it. I was already working at McDonalds at night, Foot Locker during the day, and Macy's on the weekend, but no matter how many hours I put in, it felt like the bills just kept piling up. But everything changed when my girl Honey put me on.

As I was sitting in the mall on lunch break from a hard shift at footlocker, I spotted Honey heading my way with her hands full of shopping bags. I hadn't seen her in weeks, but today she was looking like a whole other person. Her hair looked like it was styled fresh out the shop, and her clothes and heels were flawless. I tried to hide the confusion from my face since Honey was just like me, struggling to eat and survive. Now she's over here looking like a duffle bag of money, while I'm over here in my foot locker uniform, looking lame as fuck!

"Heyyy, girl!" She gleamed as she approached me.

"Hey, Honey," I said dryly as she dropped her bags on the table and chair next to me and hugged me.

"Girl! I just balled out today! A bitch 'bout to be lookin' fresh as hell at school on Monday. I heard the new J's came out today, I bet it was crazy, huh?" she asked as she sat across from me.

"Hell yeah," I replied before taking a sip of my drink.

"How many J's ya'll got left? I think I'm about to get me some!" Honey continued.

“Girl, they all sold out,” I lied.

“Oh... ok. Well I’mma stop at another mall and see if I can cop some,” she said as she looked over her freshly manicured nails.

“Girl! Where you gettin’ this money from? Didn’t you just quit yo’ job at KFC? You over here with bags on top of bags!” I said in a joking manner. Even though I was feeling some type of way.

Honey laughed. “I’m onto bigger and better things! I’m out here getting that real money, fuck a part time job!” she exclaimed.

“Oh yeah?” My eyebrow raised. “Whatchu’ doin’ now?” I asked, full of curiosity.

“Girl, I’m doing some work for Big Buck, and he keepin’ a bitch laced!” She laughed.

"Oh ok" was all I could say. I heard of Big Buck and his reputation. Shit, everyone out in Akron had heard of him since he owned one of the largest strip clubs in the city. I knew of some girls who left school and started working for him, some of them even landed them a ball player and became a basketball wife. They always said that if you wanted to do big things, then you had to come Big Buck's way. Yet I never thought of working for him, until now.

"So what all do you do?" I asked.

"Sometimes I work nights, and sometimes I do private parties, and trust me, a bitch get paid. Almost 10 g's in one night paid!"

"What?" I asked in shock. "10 g's?"

"Yes, bitch! 10 g's! I'd never make that shit workin' at a regular job. Girl, if you trying to make some real bread, then you need to come holla' at Big Buck," Honey suggested.

"Shit, I just might!" I exclaimed. "But I'm not eighteen yet. I won't be until next month," I realized.

"Girl, that's aiight. You know my cousin Keith can hook you up with a fake id until then. Shit, it's just a month. Don't let that stop you from making that money," Honey replied.

"That's wassup. How soon can he get that id for me, and can you put in a good word for me with Buck?" I asked.

"Girl, he'll get that done in two days, and fa'sho! You know I gotta put my girl on. We gotta get this money and look fly together." She smiled.

"That's wassup girl. I'm definitely down for that shit." I gleamed, anxious for my possible new job.

"Yes. You're about to make this real money, girl. Yo' life will never be the same." she said. But I never thought that I would be that heavy in the game.

~~~

The first day I met Big Buck, I looked like a deer caught in headlights. Although I heard of him and his reputation, I had never physically seen him... until now. Standing at 6'4" with smooth midnight black skin and jet black facial hair covering his face, Big Buck was an overly heavyset man with a deep raspy voice and a frightening presence. I stood in front of him as he sat at his desk, smoking a Cuban cigar. His beady eyes roamed every curve of my body as I nervously stood before him dressed in a
~~~

simple white tank top, black leggings, and my black and white J's.

"So you don't have any dancing experience, but you definitely got the body of a stripper. Niggas would love yo' ass at the club," he began before taking a puff of his cigar.

"How old are you?" he asked after exhaling smoke from his mouth and leaning back in his desk chair.

"Eighteen," I lied.

"Let me see yo' ID," he commanded. Without hesitation, I handed him my fake id.

He took a moment and studied my driver's license. "Aiight. Na'Tya." He smiled as he looked up at me.

"I like you. You gotta pretty face and a bangin' ass body for eighteen. I think we can do great things with you on our team. But I need to know. Are you willing to do whatever it takes to make these bandz?" he asked as he face hardened with seriousness.

I thought about what he said for a brief second before replying. Shit, working with Big Buck would make me more money than I would ever make working at all my part time jobs combined. I hated to see my mom struggling to make ends meet, and I hated to be working hard to barely pay all our bills, let alone to have fun. I was tired of the struggle, and I wanted more out of life. I wanted more for myself. So I looked Big Buck in the eye and said,

"I'm down for whatever."

"Good." He smiled. "That's what I like to hear. A woman who is dedicated and is about her business.

I'mma make you shine like a diamond!" he exclaimed. "From now on, you will be known as Diamond Dior," he announced.

I couldn't help but smile. "I like that."

"Good. I'll have you fill out some paperwork and you can start this Friday," he replied, and just like that, I started my new journey as Diamond Dior.

After three months of stripping at his club, I had a large list of regulars who would come to the club just to see me. I was making enough money to cover Mama's bills and still have bands left over to do whatever the fuck I wanted. I barely went to school during the day, and my mama thought I was working overtime during the night and weekends. As long as I was bringing in the dollars, she didn't give a fuck what I was doing. I was on a paper chase and would do whatever I had to do to get it.

Some nights me and Honey would both dance on the stage and make the whole club go crazy. They loved seeing Diamond Dior and Honey pussy poppin' high up the stripper pole and making a damn scene to remember. Niggas all over Ohio heard about us and made their way to The Kingdom Gentleman's Club to see us. We were the club's hit sensation and was now always booked for private parties. It was crazy how much my life changed in so little time. I came from nothing, and with the help of Big Buck, I became something. I was making good money, but a bitch wanted more.

Out of all the girls in the strip club, Big Buck always had a "Fab Five" team, a group of his top strippers that would do private club events, traveling events, and jobs that would make them more money than the rest of us. As soon as one of the Fab Five quit and moved to Houston, I didn't hesitate to go to Big Buck's office and make my pitch to take her place.

"Since I've started working here I've been bringing in more business and puttin' on for the Kingdom, and I want to grow with you, Buck. I want to do more for you. I want to be a part of your Fab Five. I want to go out there and make you proud," I persuaded.

Big Buck slowly took off his dark Gucci aviator frames and looked up at me with a stern face.

"I know that you are talented, Diamond, but to be a part of my Fab Five, you gotta do more than what you doin' now. This ain't no little game of who can twerk the best upside down on the pole. This is next level shit. We have a different clientele that expects more out of our team. You got to be willing to do whatever it takes and whatever is asked of you. You understand?" he asked.

I quickly nodded my head and said "yes."

"I remember you telling me that you would do whatever it takes, but I'mma put you to the test. I got to try you out before I put you on the team. If you are up to my liking, then you will be up to my clients liking, and they don't fuck with just any bitch. They have too much shit to lose. They are game changers in the city, in the state, and nationwide. You have to be a special bitch to be a part of the team, and once you are on the team, I own your ass. Do you understand?" he commanded, leaving me speechless.

Own my ass? What type of shit was this? It can't be too bad if these girls are living it large out here, owning three-story homes and driving brand new Bentley coupes and shit.

"Do you understand me, Diamond?" he repeated with a raised eyebrow.

"Yes, Buck," I said softly.

"Good. I'll text you the details of where to meet me tonight. Be there on time or you lose your chance at being on the team," he explained.

"Ok. Thanks, Buck." I smiled as I stood up and headed to the door.

"Yeah, I'll see you tonight if you serious," he replied, diverting his attention to his computer.

"You will. I promise," I said before exiting his office. I could feel the eyes of all the other bitches on me as I made my way to the locker room. Every girl in the club wanted to be on the Fab Five, so I knew they were about to flock to his office and make their pitch. Competition was about to be fierce, so I had to bring my A-game tonight. As I changed clothes, getting ready to go home, Honey made her way over to me with urgency.

"Did you hear about Kiara leaving the Fab Five?" she asked as she leaned on the locker next to mine.

"Yep! And you know I didn't hesitate to go to his office and make my move," I said as I buttoned up my blouse.

"Oh yeah?" Her eyebrow raised. "So what he say?"

"Nothin' really. Just said that he will take it in consideration," I lied. Even though she was my girl, I knew that Honey was just like all the other girls out here. She would fuck anybody over if they got in her way of making more money. So to keep the peace until I got on the team, I played my role.

"Oh. Ok..." she said hesitantly. Honey looked around the room before leaning in, whispering,

"You know that being on the Fab Five is different from working at the club, right?"

"I guess... they gotta make more money for some reason." I shrugged.

"I heard they got to do a lot more than dancing to make they bread..." she started, but I didn't want to sit here and gossip with her.

"Well they ain't gettin' locked up or endin' up dead, so it can't be that bad, Honey," I snapped. "Look, I gotta head home and chop it up with Moms about her bills 'n' shit. So I'mma holla' at you later, ok?" I said, ending this conversation.

"Ok... holla' at you later" was all she could say as I grabbed my bag and headed out the locker room. At this point in my life, I didn't want to hear what she had to say, cause I knew that as soon as I left, Honey would be right in Buck's office all up in his face tryin' to get on. So she can talk all the shit all she want to, but I was determined to get on that team and get this bread up.

Hours passed when I finally got a text from Big Buck. He wanted me to meet him at the Hilton hotel within the next hour, and I had to wear a sexy dress and six inch heels. After taking a quick shower, I slipped into an all-black Dior dress that I copped last week and some black Dior heels. I applied some light makeup and touched up my already straightened hair. I wanted to switch it up from my bright red lace front and heavy makeup to show him that I was versatile.

"You said that you were willing to do anything to get it. So tonight you better prove it," I said to myself as I hopped into my all-black Dodge Charger.

Anxiousness crept over my body as I pulled up in front of the hotel. I didn't know what to expect, but I was ready for whatever came my way. It was now or never!

After texting Buck, letting him know that I was on my way up to his room, I didn't even have to knock. There stood Buck in the doorway dressed in nothing but a black robe.

"C'mon in," he commanded.

I made my way into the large hotel room and sat in one of the guest chairs as he closed the door and walked over to me.

"I see you over here looking good as fuck," he said, licking his lips.

"With that look, my client will love having you in their presence. But I gotta see your skills," Buck continued.

"Ok. You want to sit here while I dance for you?" I asked.

"Dance?" He laughed. "Girl, you betta show me what that mouth do," he said as he took off his robe, revealing his naked overweight body standing before me.

I sat there in shock from what he expected of me. Now I wasn't no virgin by any means, but I never fucked niggas that I wasn't in some type of relationship with.

"Don't waste my time, Diamond. Show me how bad you want this," he said, breaking me out of my thoughts.

I put a seductive smirk on my face, covering up my shock, and said, "Ok, Daddy."

Getting on all fours, I crawled over to Big Buck until his thick eight inches was in my face. Without hesitation, I spit all over that dick and began jacking him off as I started sucking on his balls.

"Oh shit!" He grunted as he grabbed the back of my head and pushed his sack deeper into my mouth. "Mmm" I moaned as my tongue worked feverishly and my vibrating tongue ring led him to ecstasy. Once my lips finally wrapped around his shaft and my tongue swirled around the bottom of his dick in a figure eight motion, Buck was my bitch! Melting in my mouth. Within minutes, his load shot into my mouth and I swallowed every drop.

"Mmm, you got any more for me?" I licked my lips and smiled as I looked up at him.

"Hell yeah, Take that dress off and get yo' ass in this bed!" he demanded while pulling me up off the floor.

"Sit down, baby," I said as I pushed him back toward the bed. Sitting down at attention, Buck stared at me intensely as I seductively slipped off my dress, revealing my bare naked body. Keeping nothing but my heels on, I astraddled Buck as his hands roamed my body.

"Let me show you how I ride this dick, baby," I said as we laid back on the bed and I began to lower my throbbing pussy onto his firm, hardened member.

"Shit! That pussy so wet." He grunted as I squeezed my pussy around his circumference.

I began bouncing wildly up and down his shaft as his head connected with my g-spot each time.

"Fuck!" I screamed out in pleasure.

Taking it to another level, I spun around with the dick still inside and began twerking my ass while I rode him like no other.

"Damn! Get that shit!" He said, smacking my ass. I did just as he said, loving every minute of it. Before I knew it, Buck sat up, laying me down so that I was face down and ass up on the bed, and began hitting me from the back, pulling my hair and giving me death strokes.

"Fuck this pussy! Make me squirt!" I screamed out as I backed my ass up on him.

"Hell yeah, squirt all over this dick." He groaned as he picked up his speed, driving me crazy. Buck fucked me roughly, still hitting my g-spot, causing my whole body to quiver as I finally squirted all over him.

"Fuck! I'm finna' cum" He growled before he went deeper, pounding my pussy until satisfaction. "Cum for me, baby," I encouraged, backing up on that dick even more.

"F-F-Fuuuuck!" he yelled as finally came. Quickly, he pulled out and came all over my tits.

Stumbling over to the other side of me on the bed, Big Buck laid down, trying to catch his breath as sweat drenched his face. "Damn girl. You the shit," he said, causing me to laugh as I sat up and headed toward the bathroom to clean myself up.

Once I got back into the room, Buck sat on the edge of the bed, smoking on a blunt. "That's the shit I've been looking for, Diamond," he began.

"You just showed me that you are worth being on the team, and with a tight and wet pussy like that, you're about to make a killing on the Fab Five.

This is an escort business. Sometimes you have to fuck, sometimes you don't. Either way you get paid good money per hour. So I'll have you get started on Friday," he continued.

"Ok, Buck." I put on a fake smile. "I'm down."

"Good girl." He cupped my face. "You are going to be on the Fab Five, but you are going to be my favorite," he said before pulling me onto his lap. "Now lay back on this bed and let me eat that pussy. I want to taste you," he commanded, causing me to giggle as I did as was told. Who could say no to getting some head? Shit, not this bitch!

That night, Big Buck and I developed a connection outside of work. He was rich, powerful, and ran every damn city in Ohio with his drug game. If I could keep him in my pocket, then I would be one paid and powerful-ass bitch!

~~~

Once Friday arrived, I began to rethink my decision. *Did I really want to sleep with men for more money? I didn't want to end up being on the seven o'clock news because I got arranged to be with a serial killer. All it takes is one time... one bad move and I'm done.*

Haunting thoughts filled my head as I sifted through my closet, searching for something sexy to wear. I had already went this far with Big Buck to get on the team, so there was no turning back now. Time was of the essence, and I only had twenty minutes before I met with the man who paid for my time. I quickly slipped on my royal blue, curve-fitting dress and matching heels. My long black hair was loosely curled and my makeup was on point. I normally didn't dress like this, all bougie and shit, but I'm actually liking this new look.
~~~

Grabbing my clutch off the dresser, I made my exit. Mom was locked in her room as always, sleeping her life away. The only way she knew how to cope with her depressing-ass life. I got tired of seeing her like this, acting as if she couldn't get out here and get this money for herself. Once I get this money up, things were going to change.

Money made me come by Rick Ross blared through my speakers as I sped down the highway. At this point of my life, I was on that money tip, doing whatever I had to do for money. And tonight would be the first night I would have to sleep with strange men for money.

"I'm here." I spoke into the phone as I nervously bit my nails.

"Good," Big Buck replied. "He is in room 508. Don't be shy, baby. Just do what you did for me and you'll be all right," he continued.

"Ok. I'll call you when I'm done," I said as I looked around the parking lot.

"Aiight, baby," Buck chimed in before hanging up. I took a deep sigh before hopping out of the car and making my way into the Hilton Hotel. My pulse raced as I approached room 508. I felt like turning around and running back to my car, but I reminded myself why I was here in the first place.

My hand trembled as I knocked on the door. Within minutes, the door opened and the sight before my eyes took my breath away. The man that stood before me was beyond handsome. Standing at 6'3", his smooth brown skin glowed underneath the luminescent lights. All I could see were his abs and a defined v-cut and an erect dick peeking through his silk red pajama pants. I quickly glanced back up at his face and almost melted in my panties. His hazel eyes pierced my soul as they connected with mine.

He was everything I wanted and more. His curly black hair was freshly lined up, as well as his facial hair. He flashed me a warming smile, revealing his pearly white teeth and deep dimples piercing his cheeks. *Shit, fucking him would be no problem. This would hardly count as work for me, and he was packin'! This would be nothing but pure pleasure for me.*

"Hello." His deep voice broke my thoughts.

"Hi. I'm Diamond." I finally spoke.

"Ah, yes. Please, come on in," he said as he moved back and allowed me to walk into his executive suite. I looked around in awe. This room was plush. He must have major money to get this.

"Please, have a seat and make yourself comfortable," he suggested. Without hesitation, I sat on down on the leather L-sectional couch stationed in front of a 70" inch flat screen TV.

"Would you like a drink?" he asked as he made his way behind the kitchen counter.

"Sure." I smiled.

"What would you like?" he asked.

"Whatever you're having."

"Good choice." He beamed, causing me to chuckle.

"I'm a simple man. Henny and coke is all I need in this world of sin," he said with a charming smile that made me melt again.

"Nothin' wrong with that, sir." I shrugged. It was killing me that I couldn't ask this sexy man his name, but according to Big Buck, it was against the rules.

"Please, call me Travis," he said as he headed over to me and handed over my drink.

"Ok, Travis." I smiled.

"So let me ask a question..." he began as he sat down next to me.

"Go for it." I took a sip of my drink.

"What is a pretty girl like you doing a thing like this?" Travis asked as he gazed at me with his intense eyes.

I shrugged in response. "I had to do what I had to do."

"I see." He nodded.

"Can I ask you a question?"

"Sure." He leaned back onto the couch.

"What is a handsome man like you, doing a thing like this?" I asked, shocking myself by even asking him that. I knew damn well it wasn't none of my business, but there was something about him that made me feel so open.

"Good question." He smirked. "I wanted to try something different. Most women want to sleep with me based on my looks and profession. I get tired of playing cat and mouse. Always watching my back and worrying about women's motives to set me up and trap me. Sometimes I want to get straight to the point. No bullshit. A lot of my acquaintances told me about Buck and his Fab Five. Give things a try. So I finally did, and now I can say that I'm a lucky man to have you in my presence, Diamond," he explained, causing me to smile at his compliment.

“Oh really?”

“Yes. I’m not your typical client. Sometimes I just want to talk. We all need a release from our realities. Just from our interaction we’ve had so far, I know that I’m going to like you. I want you to feel comfortable around me. We’re both nervous, so this drink was just our warm up,” Travis said.

“How about I order room service and we can unwind and talk some more?” he suggested.

“Ok.” I nodded my head in agreement. Within the next five minutes, room service arrived with our food set on a table covered with a white table cloth and lit some candles, giving me the vibe of a candlelit dinner. I savored every bit of my delicious meal as we talked and shared more about each other over our private dinner.

As the night came to an end, we laid in the bed. I was dressed in nothing but my bra and panties, and he was in his boxers. Wrapped in his arms, Travis held me close and began to kiss on me. I closed my eyes and enjoyed the moment as he made his way to my wetness below. The pleasure he served me was beyond belief. That night we had the most passionate sex I had ever experienced in my young life. Ever since that day, he became my ongoing client. Soon he became more than just a client.

Present day:

Thoughts of Travis filled my mind as I watched everyone make their exit out of my house and head to their calls. *Shit, this was the perfect time to go see him,* I thought to myself as I waved goodbye to my crew. Closing the door behind me, I made my way back to my table, grabbed my cell phone, and dialed his number.

"Hello, Ms. Na'Tya," he greeted, calling me by my first name.

"Hello, Mr. Black." I smiled.

"What's going on? You don't call me unless something is going on," Travis said.

"I want to see you.... It's been a rough-ass day." I sighed into my phone.

"I'm sorry that you're not having a good day, baby. I'll meet you at the suite in ten minutes."

"Ok," I said before we hung up.

With my phone and keys in my hand, I hopped into my 2015 Mercedes coupe and made my way to my destination. Seeing Travis's sexy ass was all I needed after a day like today. As soon as I walked into the executive suite at the Hilton, there stood Travis looking sexy as ever in his black suit. Without hesitation, I jumped on his sexy ass, wrapping my legs around his torso as he gripped my phat ass with his large hands.

"Damn, I missed you," he whispered before kissing me again with his pillow-soft lips.

"Show me." I whispered back.

Tossing me onto the large bed in the master room, Travis got on top of me and damn near ripped my clothes off. Placing my thick legs above his shoulders, he buried his face inside my pussy and began to dive in with his tongue, sending pleasure throughout my body. That was one thing I loved about him, he always made sure to meet my needs first. After a mind-blowing orgasm, Travis shoved his thick ten inches deep inside me and made me forget about all my problems from the day.

After three hot and steamy rounds, I laid in the bed smoking a blunt and sharing with him how bad my day was.

"Yeah, that is fucked up that your moms did you like that," he chimed in.

"I know." I exhaled.

"It seems like there is something else bothering you, 'Tya. Is there anything that you need? Anything that you want me to do?" Travis asked, full of concern.

"Nah, boo, I'm good." I smiled.

Travis observed me with his eyes, as if he was trying to detect what was really going on with me before hesitantly nodding his head. “Ok ’Tya.... You know that I’m always here for you when you—” he began, but was abruptly interrupted when my phone rang loudly. Quickly grabbing my phone off the nightstand, I saw Buck’s name scrolled across the screen.

“Hold on, babe, let me get this,” I said urgently before hopping out the bed and heading to the living room area of the suite.

“Wassup?” I answered.

“You got a client tonight at the Sheraton,” Buck said hastily.

“Well I’m busy.” I rolled my eyes.

"What the fuck you mean, busy?" He snapped into the phone.

"I'm doin' something right now, so I'mma busy for the night."

"Bitch! Don't nobody give a fuck if you busy. When I say you got a client, then yo' ass better be ready," he yelled. " Yo' ass betta' go make me some fuckin' money or I'mma have to come drag yo' ass and slit your fuckin' throat myself," Buck threatened, making me realize who the fuck I was messin' with. Just three weeks ago, the body parts of one of the members from the Fab Five was found in the lake. Hearing him tell me this reminded me that there was only one way out this life, and I didn't want to die tonight.

"Aiight. I'm sorry, Buck. I'll be there." I sighed.

"You damn fuckin' right yo' ass is gonna' be there," he clapped back. "I arranged you to meet in the next thirty minutes, so yo' ass better not be late," he continued.

"Yes, Buck," I obeyed.

"Good" was all he said before hanging up in my face.

I threw my phone onto the couch out of frustration and sat back with my hand on my head.

"Fuck!" I yelled out.

"I heard the whole conversation, 'Tya. Why you still dealin' with that shit? You're better than this," Travis said as he leaned against the bedroom doorway.

"Easy to say coming from a married man with a fuckin' career!" I snapped.

"Look, I care about you, ok?" Travis replied, while making his way over to me on the couch. "That line of work you been doing is dangerous. My men have been tracking Buck down for the past two weeks. There are plenty of women from his club that has been missing. I'm not going to let you become the next one," he explained. Travis was the chief of police and had many connections. If anything were to happen to me, I knew Travis would be all over Buck's ass.

"I hear you, Travis. But as of now, I gotta get ready to go to the Sheraton," I said before getting up and making my way to the bathroom.

This time Travis didn't put up a fight. After taking my shower, I came back into the room and slipped on my black sundress that I previously wore to see Travis. Grabbing my stuff and making my way toward the front door, Travis grabbed my arm, causing me to abruptly halt.

"Be safe, 'Tya. And if you need me..."

"I know. I'll call you, Travis." I nodded before making my exit.

I shook my head as I tried to hold back the tears of anger. I felt like I was trapped in this shit. But it was only a matter of time before I found a way out.

The things I do for money...

~~~

"So how much for tonight?" said the old white man that sat before me.

"13,000 dollars," I replied.
~~~

"13?" The old man almost croaked. "Buck told me it was 6,500 a night."

"Well he told me it was double for tonight," I replied, giving no fucks about his complaint. I'll be damned to only get a 30 percent cut of the money I earned. A bitch had to get paid, so I did what I had to do. Fuck Big Buck and his bullshit!

He sat there, staring at me with contemplation filling his face. "Fine." He sighed. "This better be good," he remarked.

"Oh it will be." I smiled while slipping out of my dress.

I got on my knees, stationed in front of him. "I'll do whatever you want me to do. I'm yours for the night," I said before our sexcapade began. This was going to be a long-ass night!

Na'Tiva

"I enjoyed myself with you tonight, Na'Tiva," Brandon said as we were parked in front of my sister's house.

"I did too." I smiled as I looked into his mesmerizing light brown eyes.

"Mmm." He bit his lip. "Yo' ass is so fuckin' sexy," he said with his sexy voice, causing me to instantly get wet.

Before I could say anything, Brandon smoothly grabbed the back of my neck and began kissing me deeply in one swift motion. I closed my eyes and enjoyed the passion from his kiss. I wanted him just as bad as he wanted me. The old 'Tiva would have fucked him right here in this car, but the thought of my boyfriend Damien filled my mind.

"I'm sorry," I said as I pushed him away. "I can't..."

"It's ok. I'm sorry, 'Tiva," he said sincerely as he sat back in his seat and looked at me. "It's just so hard to control myself around you.... I just missed you," he explained, causing me to smile.

"Me too. It's just... complicated." I sighed.

"I understand. Let's just take it slow. You're not in town often, so I want to spend as much time with you while I can," Brandon replied.

"I'd like that." I smiled, trying to ease of the sexual tension.

"Good." He smiled back. "Let me walk you to the door, beautiful," he suggested before hopping out of his car and heading over to the passenger side to open my door.

Taking his hand to get out the car, all I could think was how perfect this man was. After we said our final good-byes on the porch, I watched as Brandon got back in his Bentley coupe and skirted off. A pang of guilt hit me once again. How could I be falling back in love with B-Moore when I'm still involved with Damien?

Making my way upstairs to my bedroom, I pulled out my cell from my clutch and began to dial Damien's number. After one ring, my ass was sent straight to voicemail.

"This is the one and only D-man. NFL all-star! Leave me a message or get the fuck off my line..." His arrogant voice filled my ears as I rolled my eyes in frustration. I hadn't talked to him since I touched down in Akron, and he got the nerve to not even answer my calls.

"Damien, the least you could do is answer your phone. I've been out of town for a while now and we haven't had a full conversation. I miss you.... Call me back, babe," I said before hanging up and throwing my phone on the other side of the bed.

What type of boyfriend treats his girl like that? I sighed as I slipped out of my dress and began to change into my white T-shirt and pink pajama shorts.

Trying to take my mind off my complicated love life, I laid down on the plush bed and began to watch the reruns of the latest reality show on TV. After an hour passed, there was still no call back from Damien.

"Fuck it!" I snapped as I cut my phone off and tossed it onto the nightstand. Damien couldn't even call me back, yet Brandon was texting me throughout the damn show, keeping a smile on my face. As I laid in the bed thinking about what transpired tonight, I decided that I would deal with Damien when I got back to Atlanta, but in the meantime, I was going to treat myself with a dose of B-Moore's sexy ass. No fucks given and no regrets. It was time to get what's mine.

~~~

"I want to see you," I said softly into the phone the next morning.

"Oh really?" he inquired.

"Yes." I smiled through the phone.

"How about you come to my office around twelve and we can have lunch?" he offered.

"Sure. Text me the address and I'll see you then."
~~~

"Ok, cool. See you then," he concluded before we hung up.

A kool aid smile crept across my face. Things were going just as planned.

Once twelve o'clock rolled around, I walked into C&B auto headquarters dressed to kill with my red silk blouse and my black leather leggings that looked like they were painted on my thick ass. My red six-inch Colibretta style Christian Louboutin heels clicked along his marble tiled floors, as all eyes were on me in the high-rise office.

I looked around in amazement at the how professional Brandon's headquarters was, giving me Fortune 500 vibes.

"How can I help you, ma'am?" asked the blonde receptionist behind the opaque white desk.

"Hi. My name is Na'tiva Davis. I'm here to see Mr. Moore," I answered politely.

Taking a moment to check his appointments on her desktop computer, she looked back up at me with a smile. "Ahh, yes. I will have Ashley escort you to his office," she replied before picking up the phone and calling Ashley to the main floor.

Within minutes, a brunette woman dressed in a black two-piece suit greeted me at the desk.

"Hello, Ms. Davis. Mr. Moore is awaiting your arrival. Follow me this way, please," she explained.

I followed her into the stainless steel elevators and stood in silence as we made our way up to the top of the building, to the 42nd floor. As soon as we made our way to the office, there was Brandon standing in his doorway, dressed in his grey suit, looking like a sexy GQ model.

"Thank you for bringing Ms. Davis up here, Ashley."

"No problem, sir. Is there anything else you need?" she asked.

"If you could call Mr. Staudenmayer and let him know that I will be cancelling our meeting at three o'clock, that would be great," he replied as he stood in front me, oozing power and control.

"Yes, sir. Right away," she said before making her exit in the elevator, leaving us alone.

A smile covered his handsome face as his eyes roamed my curves. "All I can say is damn," he joked.

"So are you going to show me your office, Mr. Moore?" I asked flirtatiously.

"Of course. Right this way," he said, gently grabbing my hand and leading me into his large office.

Once again, I was truly amazed by how stunning his office was and how far Brandon had come along. I stood in front of his large landscape windows and took in the view of the whole downtown.

"Wow. This is gorgeous," I said in awe.

"I'm glad you are enjoying the view," Brandon said as he approached me. His arms wrapped around my waist as he pressed up on me from behind. I closed my eyes and took a deep breath as I could feel his soft lips kissing my hot spot on the back of my neck.

"Mmm..." A soft moan slipped out of my mouth as I pushed my ass back onto his now hardened dick. I couldn't take it no more. I wanted him. Right here. Right now.

"I want you Brandon," I whispered as his hands roamed my body, driving me crazy.

Turning me around, Brandon planted a hot, fiery kiss on my lips before pulling my blouse over my head and unsnapping my bra. We feverishly undressed each other in between passionate kisses. All I could see was his sexy muscular body covered with tribal tattoos and his tasty caramel dick, causing my pussy to drip even more. Dropping to my knees, I grabbed his thick eleven inches and began to engulf it in my wet and warm mouth.

"Fuck!" He groaned as he grabbed a handful of my hair, while my head bobbed up and down on his shaft. I sucked his dick so good that his knees began to buck from pleasure.

"I can't take it." He grunted as he pulled out of my mouth. In one swift motion, Brandon picked me up off the floor and laid me onto his desk after damn near pushing everything off his wooden desk.

Putting my legs around his shoulder, Brandon slowly inserted his hardened member inside of me, making my body quiver. Pleasure filled my body as Brandon gently choked me while pumping in and out of my wet pussy. With every stroke, he hit my g-spot over and over again, causing me to cum repeatedly.

"Shit. I'm about to cum," he breathed out.

"Mmm. Cum for me, baby," I moaned as he picked up his speed, fucking me into a frenzy until we both came in unison.

"Damn, I missed you," Brandon said after we cleaned ourselves and up and were getting dressed.

"I know." I smiled.

"So how about lunch?" He chuckled as he wrapped his arm around me and escorted me out of his office.

"I thought you would be busy today? With work and all?" I asked in confusion.

"I run this business. I can come and go when I please. I can work any other day, but spending time with you is a one in a million," he said sincerely, looking me dead in the eye.

I couldn't help but smile in response, feeling like a schoolgirl all over again.

"I'd rather spend the rest of the day with you then sit in boring meetings," he continued.

"I can understand that. So where to?" I asked as I stepped into the elevator.

"Don't worry about all that. Just know I got something nice in mind." He gleamed, flashing me that flawless Colgate smile.

Excitement surged through my body as we sat in the backseat of the black Rolls Royce limousine that his personal driver pulled up in. I couldn't take it any longer. Curiosity got the best of me.

"Where are we going, Brandon?"

"I knew you couldn't hold out any longer." He laughed. "We are going to one of my estates in Pepper Pike."

"One of your estates?" I asked, impressed.

"Yes. I have five estates, even one in Avon Lake, and Gate Mills," he chimed in, naming places that had four and five million dollar properties.

After a long drive, we arrived at his immaculate estate. I was in awe as he showed me around his eleven-bedroom mansion. Once we got to his large deck outside, I was greeted by a large table covered with a white table cloth, set with gorgeous roses in a vase.

I loved the whole ambiance as his servers presented us with a gourmet meal. As we sat there holding hands and gazing into each other's eyes after we ate our lunch, I realized just how much I had loved this man during my teen years, and that I needed to actually give him another shot.

"I don't want you to go," Brandon said sweetly.

"I don't want to go either."

“How about you stay the night.... I would love to just hold you in my arms, just like the old times,” he suggested, tugging on my heart strings even more. Damn, I loved this man. Without hesitation, I agreed.

Brandon had finally become the man I’ve been wanting, and as of today I knew that my life would never be the same. I may have left him in the past, but I’m not about to leave him... not now, not ever.

Na'Tya

I woke up the next day in the Sheraton suite alone. The old white man I had entertained for the night was long gone, and the envelope with my nights pay was laid out on the table. Sitting up with my hair tangled, I grabbed the envelope and thumbed through the big-faced bills, making sure that I got every dime of my money.

Placing the envelope full of money back on the night stand, I made my way to the bathroom where I enjoyed the hot steamy shower, washing away every trance and stench of that man. I was determined that last night would be my final night in this escort business. Travis was right, I am better than this. I mean, shit, I paid my dues. I'll always appreciate the opportunity Buck presented me when I was struggling to make ends meet. But as of now, things gotta change. I got my money stacked up, I'm living nice, and I'm making my own money.

Without shaking ass and sucking an old white man's dick and balls. It was time for a change.

Thoughts about what's next in my future flowed through my mind while I hopped out of the shower and began to oil myself up. I quickly slipped into my Victoria's Secret sweat outfit that I had packed in my overnight tote bag. I pulled my hair up into a high bun, and a bitch was ready to go. Grabbing the envelope filled with cash, I stuffed it in my bag before I made my way out of the hotel room to my car.

Plugging my phone into the car charger, I realized I had over ten missed calls from Buck. I sighed in annoyance at the fact that he was blowing my phone up like this! I didn't have time to hear his mouth about shit, so I tossed my phone onto the passenger seat and pulled out of the parking lot. I don't ever want to see the Sheraton no more, and I for damn sure don't want to hear from Buck after today.

Since my stomach was growling, I stopped at a local breakfast joint to get some good food. As I sat there, waiting for my meal, a text message popped up on my phone. The message was from Big Buck, and without even having to hear his voice, I knew this text message was filled with rage.

Where the fuck are you with my money bitch! was spread across the screen.

I shook my head as I shoved my phone into my purse just as the waitress walked up with my plate of food. *Fuck Big Buck! I'll deal with his ass when I'm good 'n' ready,* I thought to myself as I devoured my food. After ruining my night after I was already having a fucked up day, I could care less if he waited on his cut of the money!

After fully enjoying my meal, I paid the bill and walked out in a better mood. A smile crept over my face as I was cruising down the streets toward the crib. I had other things to do than to worry about Big Buck. Tonight was my night to host the biggest party at the strip club tonight. And maybe then I'd give Buck his cut of the money. If not, fuck it!

Once I finally got to the crib, I noticed that 'Tiva still wasn't there. I guess her and B-Moore was fucking and catching up for old times' sake.

Making my way into my bedroom, I grabbed my lighter and rolled up blunt off my dresser. It was time to spark up and calm my nerves. I laid down on my plush bed, once again trying to regain my energy for tonight.

~~~
~~~

Rae Sremmurd's "Throw some mo" blasted throughout the club as I stood on the stage, smackin' ass and making it rain on the strippers.

"Turn the fuck up!" I yelled into the microphone as the large crowd went crazy. The event was in full swing, all the big name people were in the building. The large strip club was jam packed and a bitch was about to get paid by the two party promoters that offered me to host this event.

"All right ya'll, give it up for my bitch, the baddest bitch in the city... other than me. Give it up for my bitch Honey!" I yelled out, making the whole club go crazy.

While Honey took the stage doing her crazy performance, I stood by the bar sipping on my drink when Big Buck made his way over to me. Wrapping his arm around my waist, he pulled me close into his body. Playing my role, I pretended not to notice the scowl plastered on his face.

"Come to my office, now!" Big Buck barked into my ear. Not allowing me to have a choice, Buck gripped my arm as he drugged me through the crowd of people to his office. Flinging me into the chair in front of his desk, Big Buck towered over me.

"Where the fuck is my money!" he yelled.

"It's right here," I retorted as I fished the money out my bra and slapped it onto his desk. Buck pick up the money and thumbed through it, counting each bill carefully.

"Where the fuck is the rest?" he snapped.

I sat there confused at his statement before speaking again. "What you mean where is the rest? It's all there."

Big Buck let out a chuckle before continuing. "So you 'bout to run game on me like I don't know you been taxing customers?"

I sat there speechless, trying to figure out how he knew. My mouth grew dry as the wild look in his eyes intensified.

"Don't look shocked now, I been knowing for months that you been taxing customers, and the fact that you thought you could hide this from me is laughable!" Big Buck spat before he grabbed me up and fished the rest of the money out of my bra.

"Give me back my money!" I screamed as he tossed me to the ground.

"Yo money? Bitch, you lost yo' fucking mind! Every dime you make is mine!"

A scowl formed on my face as rage filled my body. I stood up in anger, forgetting about the fear of knowing the he killed off many of the women in his Fab Five. But I didn't care anymore! I worked too hard to get that money, and the fact that I had to step on so many people's toes just to have his fat ass take my money wasn't cutting it.

Cocking my arm back as far it would go, I slapped Buck across his face! Before he was able to recover from the shock, I kicked him in the balls, causing him to topple over in pain. Grabbing my money and stuffing it back into my bra, I ran out of his office and pushed through the crowd of people in the club.

Finally making it to the exit, I ran toward my car. But without even realizing that Big Buck was on my tail, he grabbed a handful of my hair, stopping me in my tracks. No matter how hard I tried to fight him off, he was still able to drag me back to the alleyway. Hemming me up against the wall, Buck choked me with so much force causing me to rapidly lose my breath.

Tears filled my eyes as I clawed at his hands. He began to slap me over and over again as his grip tightened around my neck. Even though my vision was starting to blur, I still managed to see him reaching for his gun that was stationed on his hip. It was now or never. With me reaching the last bit of my breath and my time coming to an end, I reached for my knife that I had strapped under my dress and slashed Big Buck across his face.

He instantly let go of my neck, causing me to drop onto the cement parking lot. Gasping for air, I gripped the blade and rammed it into his fat stomach, stabbing him over and over again. Blood gushed from his wound and spilled all over my hand. Screams of agony filled the air as he slumped onto the ground. But his screams were overpowered by the blurring music of the club.

Big Buck's body laid on the ground, lifeless, as I rose to my feet. Hacking up some spit, I spat on his fat corpse, yelling, "Fuck you, you fat bitch!" With those words leaving my lips, I felt a rush of relief fill my body.

Exiting the alleyway, I made my way to my car. Luckily no one was in the parking lot. Everyone was still in the club, even the security guards. Popping the trunk, I pulled out a towel and wiped the warm blood off my hands. With my hands still stained with Buck's blood, I hopped in my car and sat there for a moment when the reality of what I had just done hit me like a ton of bricks. I had to get the fuck outta here!

Adrenaline still pumped through my body as I sped out of the parking lot and hopped on the highway. Without a second thought, I called Travis.

"I fucked up. I fucked up bad, Travis."

"What's wrong? What you do?" he said urgently.

"I-I killed him!" I cried. "He tried to kill me and I killed him."

"Buck?"

"Yes.... I-I don't know what to do, Travis. He had me in the alleyway. He was choking me and slapping me. I was on the ground and I just knew he was about to pull out his gun. I had to do something..."

"Where were ya'll at?"

"In the alley by The Kingdom Strip Club."

"Where are you now?" he asked.

"I'm on the highway heading home."

"Good. Go home and stay there. I'm about to have my men come and clean this shit up. Just stay at the house. I'll call you when we get this shit fixed," he demanded.

"Ok," I said before we hung up.

As soon as I made it back home, I took a shower, scrubbing off Buck's blood. To get rid of the evidence, I cleaned off the knife with bleach water and threw my clothes that I wore tonight in my fireplace. Taking a deep sigh of relief, knowing that Travis would handle this mess, I laid in my bed and dialed another familiar number from my backup phone.

"Hello." The deep voice filled my ears.

"I did it, baby. I got rid of that mothafucka' and I got Judge Corgan to clear that case for you." I gleamed.

"That's wassup, baby. We about to take over the game now."

Chapter Six

Na'Tiva

After spending the night with Brandon, I decided to stay an extra two weeks in Ohio. This time, instead of staying with my crazy sister, I stayed in one of Brandon's mansions. Every moment spent with him kept getting better and better. Who would have thought that we would reconnect again? Especially on this level. All I wanted to do was stay in bed, make love to Brandon, and cuddle with him until we went to sleep. I forgot all about school, work, and even my relationship with Damien. But as the weekend approached, I figured that I needed to return to my old life in Atlanta until I graduated. Then I could move back up here with Brandon.

Tomorrow, I would take the flight back to Atlanta and take care of the things that needed to be handled, but tonight, I was going to spend my last night with Brandon. He said he had something special planned for me, so I slipped into my sexy black dress and matching heels, and my diamond studded necklace that he bought me last week. After curl wanding my hair and applying my makeup, I was ready to go!

I came downstairs only to see Brandon standing by the front door, looking as sexy and dapper as always. He was dressed in a black tuxedo and silver tie this time. Damn, I loved that man!

"I can't wait for you to see what I have planned for your sexy ass tonight." He licked his lips as he pulled me close to him.

"Mmm... well I can't wait 'til we get back home and really have some fun," I said before kissing him on the lips.

"Ooo, I can't wait." He smiled and grabbed my hand, leading me out the front door.

Our night started out with dinner at an extravagant five-star restaurant. Following that, we made our way to a star-studded party hosted at an upscale nightclub.

Brandon and I danced the night away at the club. The whole time he made sure that this would be a night I would always remember. After dancing to five songs straight, Brandon and I made our way back to our private VIP section.

Brandon ordered the most expensive champagne the club had to offer, and within minutes the shot girls came up the stairs with two 30 liter bottles of

Armand de Brignac Midas champagne, topped with sparklers in them. A big smiled crept over my face as the shot girls pranced around us with the bottles in hand. At that very moment, I felt like a princess. Going back to Atlanta was the last thing on my mind. Shit, if it was up to me, I would say fuck everything else and just stay with Brandon for the rest of my life.

As the night finally came to an end, Brandon and I made our way to his luxury truck. Feeling the many drinks that we had back at the club, I rested my head against the cool window as he drove down the street. Stopping at the red light, Brandon reached over and grabbed my hand, lacing his fingers in mine.

"You okay over there?" he asked as he brought my hand to his lips and began to kiss each fingertip.

"Mmmhmm, just a little drunk right now," I stated while looking over at him.

"I told you that you can't hang with the big dogs!" He chuckled.

I laughed in response and looked back at the red light, which seemed to be taking forever to turn green. There we sat in his truck, the only ones on the street with no traffic coming in either direction. This moment seemed so surreal.

Suddenly bright lights pulled up, blinding us from behind. Raising my hand to block the light shining in my eye, I turned around slightly and saw a truck inching closer and closer upon us, as if they were about to hit us.

"What the fuck?" were the only words I could get out before another truck screeched beside us, the passengers rolled their windows down and quickly released a whole clip into Brandon's truck.

I screamed uncontrollably as bullets ripped through the car, hitting Brandon and shattering glass, sending pieces of the truck all over the place. Brandon hit the gas pedal, sending the truck flying forward into the middle of the intersection.

Time seemed to go in slow motion as the bright lights of an oncoming vehicle came closer to my side of the car and smashed right into the truck. The vehicle T-boned our truck so hard that it sent our car tumbling. The car rolled over until it stopped upside down.

Fear gripped my throat as I sat there, stuck in my seat, with glass everywhere. Brandon, still in his seat belt, laid there wounded and covered in blood. Pain shot through my body as I tried with all my might to get out of the truck, but my body went limp. My breath slowed as my vision got blurry. Before I blacked out, I saw a man reaching into the truck, pulling Brandon's body out of the car. I reached out to the man to say something, but nothing came out of my mouth. I felt like I was paralyzed and quickly slipping away. Next thing I knew, everything was black.

~~~

The slow and steady beeps of a machine was the first thing I heard upon opening my eyes. I was greeted by blinding white fluorescent lights and the stench of staleness. My eyes finally were able to make out my surroundings when a gentle, soft hand gripped mine. My sister's tear-drenched face hovered over me. Confused, I tried to reach out to comfort her, but pain surged throughout my body. I tried to speak, but nothing came out.
~~~

"Someone please get the doctor in here! My sister is awake!" Na'Tya screamed frantically.

She looked back down at me before clenching my hand and spoke slow and softly. "Everything is going to be ok, Tiva. You've been in a coma for six months."

Coma? I've been in a coma for six whole months? I thought to myself, trying to make sense of the information that my sister just revealed to me. The doctor rushed in and started to remove the tubes that were shoved down my throat, which previously were there to help me breath. While one doctor was taking care of my many tubes, another doctor was flashing a bright light into my eyes and checking my vitals.

Finally free from the tubes, a dry pain increased in my throat. I tried many times to speak, but still nothing. Na'Tya handed me a cup of water and I slowly tried to drink, but even that was painful.

"Do you remember anything that happened to you?" The doctor asked as he stood in front of my hospital bed.

I laid there trying to recall what exactly happened that night, but there was nothing. All I could vaguely remember was being out with Brandon and sitting at the light. Then after that, total blackness. I looked at the doctor and slowly shook my head no to answer his question.

"Well it isn't odd that someone who has been in a coma for six months will forget certain things. So just rest up and we will continue this conversation later," he explained. I just shook my head in agreement as he made his exit.

I looked at Na'Tya and struggled to speak once again, and this time even with the dry pain in my throat, I was able to partially get out what I been trying to ask Na'Tya since I woke up from this coma.

"B-B-Bran..." I stammered, struggling to get Brandon's name out of my mouth. Na'Tya grab my hand and shushed me as she began to talk.

"'Tiva, you have no idea what has been going on since you been in a coma. So I'mma fill you in on everything. First and foremost, Brandon is gone... vanished without a trace. When they found you at the site of the car accident, his body and any traces of him was gone. Same with you. The person who did this to you took everything in your wallet, including the little bit of cash you had," she disclosed.

I laid there and shook my head in disbelief of the fact that Brandon was gone. Tears filled my eyes as I started to silently cry at the thought that Brandon could possibly be somewhere dead. But Na'tya wiped my tears before continuing.

"Don't cry for that fuck nigga! He is the one that did this shit to you, 'Tiva! The streets been talking ever since you been in a coma. They claim that a rival drug lord was plotting on killing him, so he faked his own demise, hiring someone to perform a shootout and rob him before grabbing him out the car and kidnapping him. And to make matters worse, what he did to you was all a part of the plan!" Na'Tya yelled out of rage.

There were no words to describe the emotions I was feeling right now. Why was hurting me a part of Brandon's plan?

Not wanting to hear anymore, I rolled over in the hospital bed, away from Na'Tya, and closed my eyes as I cried quietly to myself. *What the fuck was going on?* was all I could think, over and over again, before I drifted off to sleep.

The following months after waking from my coma have been nothing but hell. The emotion of sadness was gone and replaced by rage. Finding out that Brandon set me up was one thing, but what came after was far worse.

Investigators that were working on my case came to me many times with new information. First, the fact that my identity was taken and was being used by a woman named Kayla. At first the investigators didn't think that this and the car accident case were connected, but later it was revealed that Kayla was Brandon's ex-girlfriend, who went missing a couple of weeks after the car accident.

The second time the investigators came to me, they informed me that they found out that this

Kayla woman had drained my savings and checking account and even opened a few credit cards in my name, which were also maxed out. They had reasons to believe that Brandon was alive and well and was with Kayla. All this was pinpointed in a location overseas, so they were out of jurisdiction. Unfortunately they could only do so much as far as my identity was concerned.

The fact that this could take months to fix caused me to slip into a great depression. To make matters worse, my job terminated me and the school suspended me since I missed well over half of the term. To top all that off, my NFL boyfriend, who didn't even seem to care that I was out of town, hadn't made any attempt to see me or be concerned that I was in a coma. This mothafucka' even had the nerves to prance around on TV with his new woman like I never even existed.

In the last months of my hospital stay, I began extensive physical therapy. I was slowly able to move and walk, but I would still need assistance and ongoing sessions after discharge. But even though I regain all that, it all came with a price. Even with all the surgery the doctors did to fix me, the damages that Brandon caused me that night was too great.

“Now, Ms.Davis, I don't want you to be alarmed by the damages. I can reassure you that wounds like these can be fixed. Unfortunately, the surgeries will be expensive,” the doctor warned before placing a mirror in my hand.

“How much money are we talking?” Na’Tya questioned.

“With the extent of your damages, if you had insurance, it should roughly cost about 20,000 dollars. But without insurance, you are going to come out of a lot of money.”

The anticipation filled my body as I held on to the mirror tightly, but the horrible reflection that I saw would forever be etched into my memory. As the doctor slowly unraveled the bandages from my face, nothing in this world could have prepared me for what looked back at me.

There in the reflection was a disfigured me. Deep scars filled my once beautiful, flawless face. I looked like a fucking monster! I threw the mirror onto the floor and sobbed uncontrollably. Na'Tya tried her best to comfort me, but it was no use. Every ounce of confidence I had was now gone. I had purely and utterly nothing in this world, and to me, death sounded real nice.

To think that during my whole life, I worked so damn hard to achieve everything that I knew I deserved, just for it to be ripped away in a matter of seconds! All because I actually thought there could be something between me and Brandon. I was such a fucking fool to think that I could find true love! Everything in my gut told me not to come back to Akron. But against my better judgement, and for the sake of my late mother, I still came and risked everything.

~~~

Since today was discharge day, 'Tya came to my room with clean clothes for me to change into. I sat on the hospital bed, holding back tears as 'Tya helped me get into a plain grey T-shirt and some sweat pants. It pained me that I had to be so dependent on my sister, especially after our rocky history and my years of independence. No one said a word to each other as the nurse came into my room with a wheelchair. I felt so weak as both my sister and the nurse helped me get into the wheelchair. It would still take time for me to walk normal, even with the physical therapy.
~~~

'Tya and I remained silent as she pushed me in the wheelchair.

"Let me go get the car, 'Tiva," my sister said once we were outside the hospital entrance.

I nodded my head to let her know it was ok before she made her way to the parking lot, leaving me sitting in my wheelchair.

As I sat there reflecting on all that had happened to me, pure animosity filled my body. How many times has love fucked me over and brought me down? How many times did I have to learn the hard way? Everything I had was gone. My beauty, my money, and almost my life. All for a thing called love.

I could feel myself growing colder day by day. At this point in my life, my motto was "don't love no one, don't trust no one." The only person in this world that I could trust was my sister, who had been by my side despite our differences.

I swear, I'mma find that fuck nigga and kill him and all those affiliated with him. Prissy little Na'Tiva is dead and gone, time for the new me to come alive and seek my revenge. They say karma is a bitch, and that revenge is best served cold. But fuck all that! I'm making my own rules, and with these rules there will be blood...

~~~

Find out what happens next in
I Am The Streets part two! Available Now!
~~~

I AM The Streets 2:

After the drastic event that leaves Na'Tiva permanently scarred, she is willing to do anything she can to get her revenge. Now that Buck is out of her way, Na'Tya is determined to build her empire. Yet everything is not as easy as it seems when the two face a new set of problems.

Find out what happens in part two of
I AM The Streets! Available Now!